One Act

The Affair

&

Lavender's Blue

Two
One Act Plays

Zaid S Sethi

Copyright © Zaid S Sethi 2022

This book is sold subject to the condition that it shall not by way of trade or otherwise, be lent, resold, hired out, or otherwise circulated without the author's prior written consent in any form of binding or cover other than in which it is published and without a similar condition including this condition being imposed on the subsequent purchaser. All the characters in this book are works of fiction.

Any resemblance to any individual, dead or alive is coincidental.

For Gretchen, Daniel & Marianne

By the same author

Novels

Faith, Hope & Love
Paris

Short Story Collections

The End of the World
The Dream of Angels
The Loneliness of Love
Blue Tomorrows

"A problem is only insoluble to the sufferer; to others, it may have a comic or exasperating simplicity." Sebastian Faulks, *Where My Heart Used to Beat*

"One day I will find the right words, and they will be simple" Jack Kerouac, *The Dharma Bums*

Introduction

Here are two one act plays which were commissioned by friends to help them with their business ventures. For the friend who commissioned *The Affair,* it was his starting out as a restaurateur and was intended to be used at the launch of the restaurant, and *Lavender's Blue* was commissioned by a friend who had an entertainments company which had a side business running speed dating events.

The Affair

Two married people in their forties (a man and a woman) meet for dinner in a restaurant.

We meet the two people in the middle of a conversation, just as they've finished their main course. Their conversation during the course of the play is interrupted by a telephone call from the woman's fifteen year old daughter, and young son, as well as two soliloquies in which each of the protagonists tell us a little of their lives outside this encounter and how they separately recall the circumstances which brought them together.

The play is called 'The Affair' to encourage the audience to bring into play their personal understanding of what it means to have an affair and, to consider whether there has been a betrayal during the course of this dinner.

The play was inspired by a short story I'd written, which is included in my short story collection *'The Dream of Angels',* first published in 2011. The production of the play was intended to form part of the entertainment where the audience is invited to have dinner which is followed by the performance which takes place at a table set in the middle of the restaurant.

Lavender's Blue

The play is about two single people in their early thirties, who are friends. The journey takes us through four scenes; the first scene introduces the protagonists at the girl's flat, the second sees them exploring the idea of attending a speed dating event which also takes place at the girl's flat, the third takes place at the speed dating event and, in the last scene, we return to the girl's flat to see how their attendance at the speed dating event has affected their lives.

The play is entitled Lavender's Blue, the title taken from the English Folk song and nursery rhyme from the 17th century. The premise of the play is from the lines of the song 'You must love me, cause I love you,' and explores whether there are circumstances in which that can be enough.

Zaid S Sethi
October 2022

Contents

The
Affair

The Affair

Duration – approx. 60 mins

Players –

> **Helen**
> **Charles**
> **Waitress**

Scene – *Charles and Helen sit at a table for two at a restaurant (seated in profile to the audience). Both smartly dressed, early forties, confident, with an air of success, it looks like they both have come straight from the office. Helen has a large handbag hanging on the side of her chair. The handbag is more practical than feminine. The restaurant is elegant but not pretentious. Lighting is subdued. There is a crisp white tablecloth over the table and two half-filled glasses of wine. The plates from the main course are lying on the table but the food has been eaten by the time we intrude on their conversation. There is a waitress standing a discreet distance from them looking away from the table. You can tell she's bored.*

Helen - 'You know, you really ought to stop saying

       things like that.'

Charles - 'Like what?'

Helen - 'What you just said.'

Charles - 'What did I just say?'

Helen - *(affecting girlish intolerance)* **'Stop doing that!'**

Charles - *(he's aware he's flirting but is acting with affected boyish incredulousness)* **'What?'**

Helen - **'Saying those things. Are you flirting with? me?'**

Charles - *(in a tone of half affected flirtation)* **'Who, me? No!'**

Helen – **'Yes you are!'**

Charles – *(a little more seriously)* **'No. Really, I'm not.'**

Helen – *(still in the same girlish mood)* **'Then what do you call this.'**

Charles – *(man pauses and then timidly)* **'I think I'm falling in love.'**

Helen – *(Helen taken by surprise, pauses – then dismissively)* **'Don't be silly.'**

Charles – *(with more confidence)* **'No, really.** *(pause)* **I think I am.'**

Helen - 'That's silly.

Charles – 'Why?'

Helen – 'I'm married!'

Charles - 'I know. So am I!'

Helen – 'We're both married!'

Charles – 'So?'

Helen – 'We're not allowed!'

Charles – 'I don't think you can just flip a

> **switch! I mean...**

(Helen's mobile telephone rings. The man doesn't finish what he was going to say. He watches her rummage through her handbag slightly irritated at not finding her phone immediately. Finds it, pulls it out of her handbag and before accepting the call looks at the number.)

Helen – *(looking up at Charles)* **'Sorry,** *(she says*

> *accepting the call and then quietly with affected*

> *apology)* **it's my daughter...**

> **'Hello,** *(pause)* **Hello darling.** *(she says smiling*

> *at the man, stops smiling, concentrating on what*

> *her daughter is saying to her. Long pause while*

she's listening to her daughter) **Which one?** *(pause)* **'I know, but which one? The blue one or the red one?** *(pause)* **No. That's alright.** *(pause)* **I know, you always look lovely.** *(pause)* **Of course you can.** *(pause)* **No I don't mind.** *(pause)* **Only, darling,** *(pause)* **yes, I know, but you will be careful. It's expensive. You remember how upset Daddy was when I got them.** *(pause)* **No, of course not. I know you're careful.** *(pause)* **No, I wasn't going to remind you about the shoes.** *(pause)* **Yes, I know that was an accident.**

(She looks up at the man as if she'd forgotten she's not alone.)

Look, darling, I can't talk now. *(pause)* **Because I'm not alone.** *(pause)* **No-one you know.** *(pause)* **No, it's not Aunty Jill, it's...a colleague from work.** *(pause) – she looks flustered at having lied, looks at the man hoping*

he hasn't heard. Charles looks away, as
if concentrating on something on the table, as if
he's not listening. Their eyes meet. He smiles)
No, darling I can't talk now. We'll have a
chat when I get home. *(pause)* **Is Daddy**
there? *(pause)* **What's he doing?** *(then quickly,*
as if interrupting) **No I don't want to speak to**
him. *(pause)* **No, we haven't had a row.**
Everything's fine. *(pause)* **Yes, promise.**
(pause) **I'll speak to him when I get home.**
(pause and then with emphasis) **I said, I'll**
speak to him when I get home. *(pause)* **I've**
got to go now. *(pause)* **Yes, I said you can.**
(pause) **What?** *(pause)* **No, I can't take it up.**
(pause) **No, I said no, that'll spoil it.** *(pause)*
It's meant to fall below the knees. *(pause and*
again, with emphasis) **I said, No!** *(pause)* **No,**
I'm not getting angry with you. Look, we'll

talk about it when I get home. *(pause)* **No, I won't be back too late** *(pause and then pleading)* **Darling, I really can't talk now. I've got to go. We'll talk about it when I get home.** *(pause)* **Yes, promise.** *(pause)* **Love you.** *(pause)* **Bye.** *(She hangs up, smiles an apology)* **Fifteen years olds can be so demanding.** *(She puts her phone away in her handbag and turns to the man)* **You don't have a daughter, do you?'**

Charles – 'No, just sons. Two of them.'

Helen – 'Well, I've got one of each. How old are yours?'

Charles – 'Old enough not to need me anymore.'

Helen – 'God, you are a sour puss!'

Charles – 'Haven't been called that before!'

Helen – *(Ignoring his response and, as if thinking out allowed.)* **'I think boys are easier than girls.'**

Charles – 'I don't know. I wouldn't have minded a

daughter.'

Helen – 'Yes, well you wouldn't have to put up with

their teens. Men never do. It's always the

mother who has to.'

Charles – 'I think it's all exaggerated.'

Helen – 'What is?'

Charles – 'Teenage daughters.'

Helen - 'Why do men always insist on having

opinions about what they know nothing

about.'

*(Charles looks at her and then moves to take a drink.
She looks at him, turns away as if ignoring him. He
has a sip of wine. Helen relents.)*

Helen – *(affecting a reluctant apology)* **'I'm sorry. It's**

just... my daughter has a birthday party to

go to on Friday and has suddenly decided

she's got nothing to wear. *(Charles nods*

conciliatory agreement while Helen continues)

I don't like her going to birthday parties in the evening.... especially those that end up in a sleep over. She's still a bit young.'

Charles – 'I know.'

Helen – 'What?'

Charles – 'Times are changing. Children grow up faster than they used to.'

Helen – 'It's easy for you to say.'

Charles – 'What?'

Helen – 'You haven't got any daughters. Boys are different.'

Charles – 'How.'

Helen – 'You don't have to worry about them as much.'

Charles – 'I don't know.'

Helen – 'You know you don't. Boys, like men, don't have to live with the consequences.'

(Helen looks at him as if asking him to agree with her.

*Charles thinks and accepting she has a point, nods his
agreement.)*

**Charles – 'Yes, I suppose you're right. Boys are
different. But...'**

Helen – 'Yes, unfortunately, I know I'm right. *(and
then as if repaying his agreement with her
without an argument about it)* **But it's true,
they do grow up a lot quicker now a days. It
wasn't like that when we were young** *(then,
realising she interrupted him)* **sorry, you were
going to say...'**

Charles – *(man considers whether he should continue
and decides against it)* **'No, nothing. I was just
going to agree with you. I suppose it wasn't
like that when I was young. But you're still
young.'**

Helen – *(Ignoring his compliment)* **'What do you mean
'suppose'? How old were you when you had
your first girlfriend?'**

Charles – 'I can't remember. **Maybe** *(looks at her as if trying to discern what she wants to hear)* ...**sixteen?**'

Helen – 'That was a bit young wasn't it.'

Charles – 'I suppose so. But we didn't do anything.'

Helen – 'I should hope not!'

Charles – 'It was just a crush. I only got my first kiss out of it.'

Helen – 'That's sweet. Who was she?'

Charles – 'A girl in my class at school. Cindy.'

Helen – *(cheekily)* 'Obviously left an impression.'

Charles – 'Yes, well, that was a long time ago. What about you?

Helen – *(laughing)* 'I never had a girlfriend.'

Charles – *(man, taken aback by her response, quickly recovers)* '**Never?**'

Helen – *(Helen looks at him, thinks for a minute about* *how she should respond, then smiling.)* **'Hmm, I'm not sure we know each other well enough for those sort of confessions!'**

Charles – *(affecting having a childish tantrum)* **'Aw...no....that's not fair! Just when we were about to get to the interesting bit.'**

(Helen smiles at him as she takes a sip of her wine.)

Charles – 'How old were you?'

Helen – 'When?'

Charles – 'When you had your first boyfriend.'

Helen – 'I don't think it's about when I had my first boyfriend...it's about...we were a lot more innocent then.'

Charles – 'Yes, I suppose we were *(and then looks at Helen wondering whether he should risk saying what he's thinking, decides to risk it.)* **but it wasn't for want of trying!'** *(He waits to* *read her reaction. Helen hesitates in replying so he continues)* **I mean we were innocent because we failed miserably at being anything else!'** *(he adds with a chuckle)*

Helen – 'Speak for yourself!'

(Charles moves back in his chair defensively and decides not to risk going any further.)

Charles – 'No, I mean, I was speaking generally. I mean... *(regaining his confidence)* **the nineties weren't exactly the fifties, were they?'**

Helen – 'Yes, well. That doesn't mean everyone was like that.'

Charles – *(sheepishly)* **'No, of course not.** *(pause)* **Sorry. I didn't mean to... I mean... I was just saying...** *(and then with a nervous laugh)* **I'm afraid this conversation is getting a little too serious, don't you think?'**

Helen – 'What?'

Charles – 'I don't know.'

Helen – 'No, say what you mean. There's nothing to

be afraid of.'

Charles – 'What?'

Helen – 'What are you afraid of?'

Charles – *(Charles unsure of what she's talking about)*

'...nothing.'

Helen – 'I mean, we're adults and it doesn't matter

to me...' *(she looks at him trying to guess*

what he wanted to say)

Charles – *(Charles thinks about what to say and*

remembers her phone call with her daughter)

'So, raiding your wardrobe, is she?'

Helen – 'What?'

Charles – 'Your daughter. Raiding your wardrobe.'

Helen – 'Oh, yes, we're about the same size, and for

the last few months she's decided that she

has two wardrobes she can choose from.'

Charles – 'Well, you know whose fault that is.'

Helen – 'What?'

Charles – 'I mean, you know whose fault that is.'

Helen – 'What do you mean?'

Charles – 'That she thinks she's got two wardrobes.'

Helen – 'Oh, go on then.'

Charles – 'It's all your fault'

Helen – *(Helen visibly unhappy with the accusation)* 'I thought you were going to say that. So, go on, Mr know-it-all, why is it all my fault?''

Charles – 'Well, look at you, for God's sake! You look wonderful.'

Helen – *(Helen slightly surprised at the remark but obviously pleased with it, smiles)* 'Thank you.'

Charles – 'You're welcome. But it wasn't a compliment. You really do.'

Helen – *(Helen looks at him for a moment as if sizing him up before she replies)* **'You're in good shape too.'**

Charles – 'No, I'm not.'

Helen – 'Yes you are.'

Charles – 'That's silly.'

Helen – 'Why don't you accept the compliment?'

Charles – 'Because it's not true.'

Helen – 'But you expect me to accept a compliment... you must work out.'

Charles – 'I'd love to say I do, but I don't.'

Helen – 'Eat sensibly then?'

Charles – 'Nothing really.'

Helen – 'Well, you're lucky. You look good for your age. I keep telling Robert to exercise but instead, he sits in front of the TV watching whatever's on or... dozing off.'

Charles – 'What about you?'

Helen – 'What?'

Charles – 'What about you? How do you manage to look so young?'

Helen – 'Thanks.'

Charles – 'No, I mean it. You really look terrific. I'd never have guessed you were a mother of a fifteen-year old.'

Helen – *(Helen looks at him and smiles and then as if she's just remembered something)* **'You really are good, aren't you?'**

Charles – 'What?'

Helen – **'Never mind.** *(Helen takes a sip of her wine but at the same time not taking her eyes off him and then changing her mind, continues)* **Why are all men such flirts?'**

Charles – 'Are they?'

Helen – 'I don't know. You're the one that started it.'

Charles – 'Started what?'

Helen – 'Flirting!'

Charles – 'I'm sorry.'

Helen – 'No, that's OK'

Charles – 'No, I am sorry.'

Helen – 'No, it's OK. Don't worry about it. I rather like it. *(Charles smiles.)* It's nice to be appreciated. A bit of harmless fun.'

Charles – 'Is it?'

Helen – *(quizzically)* 'Isn't it?'

Charles – 'I suppose it is.'

Helen – *(as if remembering something, continues)* 'What were we talking about before my daughter rang?'

Charles – *(being reminded that she's married, he becomes reflective)* 'Um, nothing really.'

Helen – 'Is everything OK?'

Charles – 'Yes, sorry. I was just thinking.'

Helen – 'What?'

Charles – 'What?'

Helen – 'What were you thinking?'

Charles – 'Nothing.'

Helen – 'What were we talking about? *(Charles looks at her quizzically)* Oh yes, I remember. It was something about falling love.'

Charles – *(Charles' face brightens up and affecting accusation)* 'So, who's flirting now?'

Helen - *(Helen laughs as she picks up her glass of wine. Her eyes are fixed on his. Removing the glass from her lips says with confidence)* 'Women have the right to flirt too!'

Charles – *(laughing)* 'Yes, I know... especially married women!'

Helen – *(laughing)* 'And married men!'

(They both laugh with affection and then in turn stand facing the audience for their respective soliloquies. During their soliloquies they interrupt their gaze at the audience with affectionate glances at each other. Their

glances show that both are enjoying the attention each is giving the other. While Charles and Helen are speaking to the audience the waitress clears away the plates and brings the dessert. Charles turns to the audience.)

Charles - 'I know why we met. I don't need to tell you she's attractive, do I? It took courage. I think you know it does.

It's easy to flirt. Especially when you're both married...safe...but, asking someone out is different. Especially when you're married. I mean there's no point. So, you have dinner. So what? I mean, and then what? Why would you? *(pause while he looks at her. Realising he is talking to the audience, resumes)* **I was surprised she said 'yes'. Women like her don't usually. Say 'yes,' I mean. I mean, yes to dinner... And she's married. It's not like we're off on a merry-go-round of illicit love. You know, off to have an affair.** *(he says in*

**Meeting on a train is a bit of a cliché but I
suppose everything becomes a cliché as you
get older. I noticed her get on. She sat next
to me. Noticed her perfume too. Didn't
really have a good look at her. One doesn't
at that time of the morning, and, anyway, I
was reading the paper. I probably wouldn't
have met her if it hadn't been for her ring
tone. It was the Simpsons. Can you believe
it! I turned to her and smiled. She smiled
back. There was a grumpy old fart sitting
next to her, frowning while she spoke on the
phone. As if to say,** *(he mimics unflatteringly,
childlike)* **'you're disturbing me'** *(continues in
his normal voice)* **just because he didn't have**

anyone to speak to. Old people are like that.
God, I hope I don't become one of those...
although she was talking louder than
she needed to. He was a bit of coward. You
know the type. The type that pick on women
and children! She didn't notice his scowl,
otherwise, I think she would've probably
said something herself. That would have
taught him a lesson!

After her telephone conversation I
complimented her on her ring tone. I did
that only to teach the coward a lesson. She
told me her son gave it to her and that could
have been the end of it. Our conversation, I
mean. But it wasn't. It wasn't just me either.
The Simpsons! Can you imagine? I hadn't
heard that ring tone before. If we grew old
together we could tell our grandchildren

it was the Simpsons that brought us together. *(he laughs)* That would be a laugh! Grandchildren! I think I'm going mad. We're married!

Yes well. It just innocent banter really. No harm done. I mean we're not famous people. You know, ones that can afford to fall in and out of love. We're ordinary folk. Lucky to have a job and a mortgage…and, of course, a family. Not the sort who'd do anything to upset the status quo. We don't take risks with what we have.

I still can't believe she agreed to come to dinner with me. I mean we both have rings… wedding rings. I mean… we talked about our children, her husband, and her job. We hide nothing because there's nothing to hide. No reason to hide anything. We're married. Married people don't have to hide anything because... we're married. We've got children... a mortgage... well, you know... responsibility. We're not young anymore. Well... we're not young enough to start all over again. I mean, why would you?

I was surprised she agreed to come to dinner. I invited her for a drink and threw dinner in for luck. This... well... this dinner, I mean... *(continues with growing confidence)* Well, it's just a dinner, isn't it? An imaginary world, something unreal, you know, two married people having dinner, flirting with each other in the safety of a public place. Too public a place for accusations of infidelity!

I was surprised she agreed. Agreed to have

dinner, I mean.

It's not as if she's a colleague who I could explain away. *(He thinks, remembers that's what she called him in her phone conversation with her daughter and then, as if the thought is unpleasant, dismisses the thought as if it's not relevant. Pauses before continuing)* **She's sweet isn't she? Like a little girl really with that little nose and the way she does her hair.** *(He smiles at her endearingly).*

Look at her! I think I could fall in love again. *'Again'* that's a strange word! It almost means that I don't love my wife anymore. But that's not true. Who says we can't love more than one person? Wonder whether I can remember what it's like the first-time round. *(thinks)* **Yes, it's wonderful to be in love. It's fun to be in love. It's fun to be**

with her.

I don't want to sleep with her. Well, that's not true. I mean, I would if I could. Wouldn't you? Maybe you wouldn't, but that's not important. I like her. It's not about sex. I mean... I suppose it is, in a way. It might be as exciting as it once was. I would be gentle. She would want me. She wouldn't move away when I touched her. She wouldn't complain she was tired all the time. Not at first anyway. But that doesn't matter. We wouldn't be together long enough to find out. Affairs don't last forever. *(pause, as if he's just heard what he said and repeats it)* Affairs.

Betrayal is an ugly word. Isn't it? That's not what this is. It's just innocent fun! We aren't going to do anything... *(he laughs)* not in the restaurant anyway! Even if we did, would it be so bad? Can't married people have fun? I'm not talking about leaving my wife...and I don't want her to leave her husband. We'll be just two people who have a harmless dinner and then go home. It's not serious. We're grown-ups, we know when to stop.

(He turns to Helen, picks up his glass of wine and takes a long, slow sip, smiles at Helen, and sits back in his chair. Helen smiles at him, takes a sip of wine, places her glass on the table, all the time looking at him, then stands, half turned, to the audience and Charles.)

Helen - 'He's a terrible flirt, but, *(looking at him with affection)* **I don't know... innocent** *(then suddenly realising what she is thinking about changes her tone to one of indignation)* **At least, I hope he is because nothing's going to happen! After all, I'm happily married.** *(Then changing to a more remorseful tone)* **I wish Robert were here instead of him. I wish**

Robert were flirting with me now. *(pauses, then turns to the Charles, looks at him as if imagining something)* **Yes, I wish it *were* him. But if it was him, he wouldn't. He did once but that was a long time ago.** *(she reflects as if remembering something)* **When I ask Robert why he doesn't say things like that anymore he laughs. Says, I'm being silly. Maybe he's right. But why do we have to grow up being sensible... I mean, I know we have to be sensible but... do we have to be sensible all the time... too tired to act as we feel? Jill, my neighbour, divorced, says all men are the same** *(looking at Charles)*. **That's so not true. I can't imagine my Robert doing what he's doing** *(Charles smiles at her, she nods acknowledgement and smiles back)*. **No, my Robert wouldn't. He's content. He's**

happy with what he gets. *(She gives a laugh, looking down at herself)* **Pity he doesn't take all he could have!**

(Looking at Charles) **He's in good shape. He's aged better than my Robert. I keep telling Robert to look after himself but he laughs me off saying his weight gives him 'presence'. Well,** *(she gives a short laugh)* **that's not what I call it when we're having sex!** *(turning to the audience)* **You know what I mean?**

(Looking at Charles) **I think he'd make a good lover, don't you? He looks the type. I wonder...** *(she looks at him as if sizing him up for something and then turns back to the audience)*

I wonder... *(she decides not to tell the audience what she's thinking).* **I wonder whether all**

men flirt! I know they do at the office. Well, the older ones... the married ones... the ones that don't stand a chance. *(With a little remorse)* There used to be more. I remember when I first started working there, God, some of them! I'm sure Robert doesn't. Poor Robert, he wouldn't know how. Anyway, even if he knew how he wouldn't. Really, you don't know him as well as I do. Well, you wouldn't of course. He's really... I mean, he's much too um... well... happily married *(and then as if remembering something, laughs)* well, except for last night. But then, as usual, it *was* his fault! If he thinks he can be insensitive one minute and then expect me to be all loving the next, he must be stupid. Arrogant pig! All I asked him to do was to turn the television down. I was trying to read through a report that had to

go out the next day and I couldn't

concentrate with the television blaring

away! He said it was *the news* as if I didn't

realise! He'd already watched it at 7

and was now watching it again at 9.

I said nothing much could have

happened in the intervening two hours. He

ignored me, making out as if he hadn't

heard.

God, I hate that! And when I repeated it, he

told me not to shout because he wasn't deaf.

He didn't stop there. He said that I should

finish my work in the office rather than

bring it home. He, can you believe it, told

me that the family comes first! As if I didn't

know that. I mean, I work for the family, too.

I don't just sit there watching TV all

evening!

I hate it when he ignores me when I'm angry, ignoring me as if I'm a child having a tantrum. And then, getting into bed he thinks I've forgotten and am happy to... well... you know... be his little 'snuggles' whenever he feels like it. God, men are so bloody insensitive!

No, he's definitely not the type. He wouldn't know where to start! I wonder what he'd say if he knew where I was now and... with him *(indicating the man she's with)* **Maybe then** he'd realise he shouldn't take me for granted. I'm still attractive. If I wasn't I would be here tonight. Well, at least he **thinks so** *(she says pointing to Charles).* He's attractive. I'll give him that. I thought so, the first time I saw him. Not young but

still... *(and then thinking)* **well, who is anymore. He is sweet, though...** *(asking the audience)* **don't you think?**

He took me by surprise when he suggested we could meet up for a drink or dinner. I joked saying if he wanted to invite me out then it would have to be dinner! It was a joke. He didn't give me enough time to realise what was happening. If he had I'd have said 'No'. I'm glad I didn't though. I can't remember when I was last out on a date. I was quite excited after I left him at the station. I felt like a little girl again. You know, being asked out on a first date. He's sweet...'

(She sits back down. Charles nods at her asking permission to top up her glass of wine holding the bottle ready to pour. She smiles indicating acceptance and he pours. She indicates him to stop and he smiles and pours an extra drop. She smiles back at him for pouring the extra drop. He places the bottle back on the table

and is just about to say something when her phone rings again. She rummages in her bag, pulls out the telephone, sees the number and smiles, and then turns to Charles.)

Helen - 'Sorry, it's my son.' *(She says apologising with affected sincerity. Charles gives her a half understanding smile while she accepts the call.)* **'Hello, darling.** *(Pause)* **Yes, I have washed it.** *(Pause)* **No, because I need to iron it.** *(Pause)* **I will iron it when I get home.** *(Pause)* **Yes, I know you need it tomorrow.** *(She listens and then with a little irritation)* **I told you not to worry. I just didn't have time yesterday after work. I'll do it when I come home.** *(pause)* **OK, OK,** *(pause)* **I said, OK!** *(getting more irritable) (pause)* **Look** *(pause)* **I said I will. I've got to go.** *(pause)* **OK, yes, I will, I promise. 'Bye.'** *(Turning to the Charles)* **'I'm sorry. Children worry about everything.'**

Charles – 'Yes, I know. But it doesn't last

forever.

(And then half telling her and half remembering with remorse) **... you know it...**

Helen – 'What?'

Charles – 'My son stopped when he was sixteen.'

Helen - 'It's different for fathers. I think fathers and sons compete. Fathers can't cope. I know my husband's already finding it hard.' *(She looks at him for acknowledgement.)*

Charles – 'Probably.'

Helen – 'I think that's why men love their work so much. It gives them the feeling of being in control.'

Charles – 'Well, we're not always in control at work either.'

Helen – 'Yes, well, why do you act as if you are when you're at home?'

Charles – 'Because you wouldn't empathise.'

Helen – 'That's not true!'

Charles – 'You don't love us for our

weaknesses.'

Helen – 'Is that why you either go into a sulk

or start a row!'

Charles – 'That's hard.'

Helen – 'But true.'

Charles - 'So, if women don't love their work,

what do you love?'

Helen – 'My children. *(After a moment's thought, adds)*

But I didn't say I don't love my work.'

Charles – 'I thought…'

Helen – 'What?'

Charles – 'Nothing.'

Helen – 'Why don't you…'

Charles – *(man interrupting her)* 'What do you like

about your work?'

Helen – *(Helen not sure for a moment what to say.*

Recovering, she continues) **'Well, it helps pay the bills. Teenagers are expensive.'**

Charles – 'I know.'

Helen – 'It's no longer possible to run a household on one income.'

Charles – 'I don't think it's been possible for a while.'

Helen – 'Well, I don't think it was like that for my parents. For example, my mother never worked.'

Charles – 'Were you well off?'

Helen – 'Not really, but somehow my father never expected my mum to work.'

Charles – 'What about your mother?'

Helen – 'What?'

Charles – 'I mean, did your mother want to work?'

Helen – 'I don't know, I don't think it ever

crossed her mind.'

Charles – 'That's very nineteen-fifties.'

Helen – 'What is?'

Charles – 'The idea of women staying at

home.'

Helen – 'No, I don't think my mother ever

wanted to work.'

Charles – 'I think working gives women

freedom.'

Helen – 'What do you mean?'

Charles – 'You know, freedom.'

Helen – 'Freedom from what?'

Charles – 'I don't know. Many things... economic

dependence.'

Helen – 'I don't think marriage is about freedom.

The whole point of marriage is that you

don't want to be free anymore. *(She thinks

about what she's just said and then corrects*

herself) **I didn't mean it like that. I mean I don't think marriage is...'**

Charles – 'I understand.'

Helen – 'I don't want to give you the wrong impression.'

Charles – 'No, that's OK, I understand.'

Helen – 'Good.'

Charles – 'So what does work give you?'

Helen – 'I feel as if I am doing something useful. What about you?'

Charles – *(ignoring the question)* **'I think we all like to feel useful.** *(then half speaking to her and half to himself)* **Yes,** *(with half a laugh)* **I felt useful once, but now all I do is what is expected of me.'**

Helen – 'Who's being nineteen fifties now?'

(she laughs, then realising her joke is not being shared becomes solemn) **'I think**

all men like feeling sorry for

themselves!'

(Charles doesn't respond. There is a pause in the conversation. Helen notices Charles staring at her.)

Helen - 'What?'

Charles – 'Your face.'

Helen – 'What?' *(She wipes her mouth and nose*

as if trying to get rid of what Charles

has noticed.)

Charles – 'No, nothing.'

Helen – 'No, tell me!'

Charles – 'You *are* beautiful'

Helen – *(Helen pauses for a moment as if deciding*

how she should react to what has just been

said.) **'You're terrible!'**

Charles – 'You're terribly beautiful!'

Helen – 'Oh stop it.'

Charles – 'No, really. You're an incredibly special

person.'

Helen – *(Helen looks away, embarrassed for a moment and then looks back at him as if she's just remembered something)* **'You know, you said you could fall in love with me?'**

Charles - **'Yes, I could. I mean...I really could.'**

Helen – **'Well, what did you mean exactly?'**

Charles – **'Nothing.'**

Helen – **'No come on. You can't just say something like that and then say 'nothing''**

Charles – **'I didn't mean anything by it.'**

Helen – **'No, of course not.'**

Charles – **'I just meant that you really are a wonderful woman.'**

Helen – *(Helen looks at him sweetly and then realising that she might be revealing something more than she should)* **'You**

mean, no longer a girl.'

Charles – 'What?'

Helen – 'I'm no longer a girl?'

Charles – 'No, that's not what I mean, and

you know it.'

Helen – 'No, I don't. Why don't you explain?'

Charles – 'All I meant was that I wouldn't be

interested in you if you were a

silly girl. That would be boring!'

Helen – 'I don't know. Men always chase

after young girls.'

Charles – 'That's a cliché!'

Helen – 'Yes, well, you would say that,

wouldn't you, being a man!'

Charles - Well, this one doesn't.'

Helen – 'Really, why not.'

Charles – 'Not everything's about sex.'

Helen – *(with a laugh)* 'I thought they had a

cure for that.'

Charles – 'What?'

Helen – 'You know... if you're losing interest

in, you know... sex.

(Charles looks at her quizzically and then, as the

penny drops, is embarrassed. Helen is affected

by his embarrassment.) **Sorry.'**

Charles – *(Charles recovers from his embarrassment)*

'No, I mean, there's

got to be something more.'

Helen – 'Yes, well, that's what we, *(she smiles and*

adds in air quotes) **'women'**, **are always trying**

to get through to you lot!'

Charles – 'No, relationships aren't about

stereotypes!'

Helen – 'Yes, well, falling in love is a

dangerous game to play when you're

married.'

Charles - 'You've become very sensible all of

a sudden.'

Helen - 'I think one of us should.'

Charles – 'Why?'

Helen – *(half exasperated and half pleading)*

'Don't joke about it.'

Charles - 'Why not?'

Helen – 'No, please.'

Charles – 'No, let's just joke about it. After

all, isn't that all married people are

left with!'

(He gives her a reassuring laugh, but a little louder than he intended. Helen looks around to see whether anyone is listening to their conversation. As she does so, she notices the waitress turns to look at their table.)

Helen – 'Shh'

Charles – 'What?'

(Charles turns to look in the direction in which Helen was looking, notices the waitress, who, as soon as their eyes meet, looks away. Charles turns back to resume the conversation.)

Charles – 'It's OK. She can't hear us.'

Helen – 'How can you be sure?'

Charles – 'It doesn't matter even if she can.'

Helen – 'Not for you, you're a man!'

Charles – 'I'm wearing a ring.' *(he says*

showing her his ring)

Helen – 'I know, so am I, that makes it

worse!'

Charles – 'Don't be silly, we could be a

married couple for all she knows.'

Helen – *(reflective, then looks at him)* 'Do you

think we look like a couple?'

Charles – 'I don't see why not?'

(They look at each other for a moment in silence.)

Helen - 'What would you do if we were...?'

(Charles smiles and instead of replying takes a slow sip of wine, all the time looking at her, thinks about saying something, changes his mind, takes another sip, returns the glass to the table and lightly shrugs his shoulders.)

Charles - 'I don't know, what would you do?'

(Helen is pensive, looking at him, she moves her hand to touch his.)

Helen - 'I don't know…'

(Helen removes her hand, takes a sip of wine all the time looking at him, places wine glass on table and with a little earnestness in her voice.)

Helen - 'Why did you want to see me?'

Charles - 'Because you're beautiful,'

Helen – 'No, seriously.'

Charles – 'I promise. That's the only reason.

> **That's what I thought from the first**

> **moment I saw you.'**

(There is a silence, It is clear to both of them that something is happening between them.)

Helen – *(Helen smiles)* **'You are very good.**

> **You must do this with every woman**

> **you meet.'**

Charles – 'Would you believe me if I denied

> **it?'**

Helen – 'I don't know. Can you deny it?'

Charles - 'But would you believe me?'

Helen – 'Maybe.'

Charles – 'OK, you're the first.'

Helen - 'You're lying.'

Charles – 'You see. Women think every man's after

one thing.'

Helen – 'That's not true. Why would we?'

Charles – 'So that you can allow yourselves

to be seduced without taking any

responsibility. You can always play

the poor naïve innocent victim.

Admit it! It's a role that women play

very well.'

Helen – *(in a patronising tone)* '**So, who's**

getting all serious now?'

Charles – *(smiles)* '**Sorry**. *(pauses, then*

changing the subject) **how's the dessert?**'

Helen - 'Sweet.'

(Helen notices man looking at the dessert.)

Helen - 'Would you like to try some?'

(Helen doesn't wait for an answer. Scoops a little onto her fork and holds it above her plate, pointing it towards the man and waits. Charles hesitates for a moment and then leans over, takes the offering but doesn't move back, all the time looking directly at her. Helen is uncertain about what is happening and then realising, smiles at him and gently pulls the fork out of his mouth. As she places her fork down in her plate she looks at her watch. Charles looks worried.)

Charles - 'What time do you have to be

home?'

Helen - 'It's OK, I'm not in a rush. Are you?'

Charles – 'No, I could stay here forever!'

Helen – *(Helen says tenderly as she moves her*

hand forward to wipe away a little

dessert left on the side of his mouth as if

were the most natural thing to do.

Charles lets her) **'You really are a**

terrible flirt!'

Charles – *(With concentrated sincerity)* 'I

promise you I'm not, sincerely.'

Helen – *(pause)* 'Then what do you mean, you

could stay here forever?'

Charles – 'It's wonderful to be with you. Why

would I want to be in a rush? The

world could go hang and I wouldn't

care!'

Helen – 'Oh please, stop it.'

Charles – 'OK, but it's just how I feel.'

Helen – 'We all feel like that about things we

can't have.'

Charles – 'Why, do you feel like that?'

Helen – 'We all do!'

Charles – 'No, that's not what I asked. Do

you feel like that?'

Helen – 'Like what?'

Charles – 'Regret about not being able to

have what you want?'

Helen – 'Regret is a hard word, don't you think? Melodramatic!'

Charles – 'So what would you call it?'

Helen – 'I don't know... something to think about when we've got nothing better to do.'

Charles – 'I suppose so.

(Pause - they both look at each other with an endearing smile but mixed with a little pain).

Charles – 'Do you wonder what your life would have been like if it had been different?'

Helen – 'Sometimes. Don't you?'

Charles – *(Half thinking to himself)*

'**Sometimes.** *(Pause)* **Would you ever change things if you could?**'

Helen – 'No. I think I have everything I ever

wanted. Would you?'

Charles – 'Yes, me too. *(Pause)* But

sometimes...' *(Charles becomes self-*

absorbed.)

Helen – 'Are you OK?'

Charles – 'Yes, I'm fine.

Helen – 'You were miles away.'

Charles – 'Sorry.'

Helen – 'No, that's OK. What happened?

Charles – 'Nothing, being silly really.'

Helen – 'What do you mean?'

Charles – 'I was daydreaming...

Sometimes... just sometimes

something happens. I don't know.

You meet someone who reminds you

what it felt like... you, meeting

you... I don't know...

*(Charles stares at Helen worrying about finishing what
he wants to say, shaking his head indicating that he is*

not going to finish what he was going to say. Helen is puzzled and then, realising what he means, hesitates, blushes. Then with obvious effort regains her composure.)

Helen – 'You're just saying that!

Charles – 'No, I promise you, I'm not.

Helen – 'If you could, would you... really?'

Charles – 'I don't know. Would you?'

Helen – 'No, of course not, but I know what you

mean.'

Charles – 'Why not?'

Helen – 'It's only because there isn't anything such

as an innocent, you know... romance.'

Charles – 'Why not?'

Helen – 'Because we are married!' *(She says*

pronouncing each word deliberately as if

losing patience with a child.)

Charles – 'I'm sorry.'

Helen – 'That's OK.' *(She says not entirely*

convinced she should forgive him but at

the same time gives the impression that she doesn't understand why she got so annoyed.)

Charles – 'No really, I'm sorry.'

Helen – 'That's OK.' *(She is still clearly unsettled)*

Charles – *(quietly, almost sheepishly)* **'I didn't mean anything.'**

Helen – 'No, I'm sorry. I didn't mean to get annoyed.'

Charles – 'No, it was silly of me!'

Helen – 'No, it's OK to ask the question, I suppose.'

Charles – 'Do you?'

Helen – 'Yes.'

Charles – 'Don't worry, married people are allowed to ask such questions.'

Helen – 'Are they?'

Charles – 'Yes.'

Helen – 'I suppose so. I don't suppose it

frightens men as much as it does

women.'

Charles – 'It does.'

Helen – 'Does it?'

Charles – 'Yes.'

Helen – 'I suppose so.'

(They look at each other as if they are wondering how brave each of them can be. Each of them searches in the face of the other for a clue as to what's going to happen next. Helen gives up, still staring at him...)

Helen - 'It's getting late. I think we should

go.'

Charles – *(regretfully)* 'Yes, I suppose so.'

(Helen takes a sip of the wine, all the time looking at the Charles as if trying to create a mental photograph of him while the man looks round for the waitress. She is still standing with her back to them. He waits for a moment, turns back to Helen as if to say he tried, notices her forlorn look, realises that it really is time to go, turns back to the waitress.)

Charles – 'Excuse me *(The waitress hears him*

and comes up to the table) **could we have the**

bill, please?'

(The waitress gives him an affected smile in acknowledgement and walks away. Charles turns and smiles at the Helen. She smiles back. Both appear to be preoccupied with thoughts of their own. They both take a sip of wine more as a distraction than any desire to drink the last of the wine. They both place the glass back on the table. Charles offers her his hand. She looks at it, hesitates and then with a quiet smile gives him her hand. He takes it in his, caressing it.)

Charles – 'You've got beautiful hands.'

Helen – 'Thank you.'

Charles – *(forlornly)* **'Yes, very beautiful hands.'**

(The waitress interrupts them. They move their hands away sharply both having been brought back to the reality of the situation. He pays the bill.).

Charles – *(Charles turns to waitress)* **'Thank**

      you.'

Waitress – 'Thank you.' *(waitress smiles a practiced*

      smile and walks off. Charles turns to the

      Helen.)

Charles – 'Where's your car?'

Helen – 'Around the corner.'

Charles - 'I'll walk you to it.'

Helen – 'No, that's alright.'

Charles – 'Why?'

Helen – 'I don't know. Maybe it's better that

way.'

Charles – *(With a little desperation in his voice)*

'You know what you said about 'an innocent

romance.''

Helen – 'Yes.'

Charles – 'Well, you know maybe… Are you

sure, I can't walk you to your car? I

really would love to.'

(Helen hesitates and, with an air of sadness, and shakes her head. She pushes her chair back before rising, as if moving away from him. Charles rises too.)

Charles – 'Thank you.' *(Helen turns to

him and he continues)* 'It was a lovely

evening.'

Helen – **'Yes,** *(and then as if speaking half to him and half to herself)* **it really was a lovely evening.** *(and with a smile and says almost in a whisper)* **Thank you.'**

(They move to the coat rack. He takes her coat and holds it for her to slip into. She turns her back to him as he slips on her coat. She turns around to find that she is standing close to him. She looks at him, he moves towards her and they give each other a nervous kiss. As she moves away from him - he reluctantly letting her go - they smile at one another, sad in the knowledge that there can't be any more. She mouths a good-bye accompanied by a girlish shy wave of the hand. He nods acknowledgement. She turns away from him and leaves the stage. He watches her go and is left alone on the stage looking in the direction in which she left, then turns with his back towards the audience, puts his coat on as the curtain falls.)

Lavender's Blue

Lavender's Blue

(Duration – approx. 60mins)

Players:

Jake

Sally

Voice over -

(Two actors, a man, and a woman, both in their thirties.

There are four scenes in total and two scene changes required during the performance; one after the second scene and one after the third scene. The first, second and fourth scenes take place in a kitchen, and the third scene takes place in a hall in which a speed dating event is being held.

A voice over is required for the third scene. Lights dim, and once the audience is hushed, the voice over of the prologue begins.)

PROLOGUE

Voice over - Once upon a time, there was a lonely

      little girl *(and affecting lament)* **sob!**

(Sally comes through the curtains lit by a spotlight which follows her as she walks over to the left corner of the stage. She turns to the audience, smiles, and gives a girlish wave.)

Voice over - Once upon a time, there was a lonely

      little girl and a lonely little boy *(and*

      affecting lament) **sob, sob!**

(Jake comes through the curtains lit by a spotlight which follows him as he walks over to the right corner of the stage. He turns to the audience with timid, perplexed expression.)

Pause

(Jake turns to notice Sally, Sally turns to Jake and, as soon as their eyes meet, they turn their backs to each other.)

Voice over - Once upon a time, there was a lonely

      little girl and a lonely little boy who

      ignored each other *(and affecting*

      lament) **sob, sob, sob!**

(Jake turns to look at Sally. Sally turns to Jake. As soon as their eyes meet, again they turn their backs to each other.)

Pause

Voice over – Once upon a time, there was a lonely little girl and a lonely little boy who continued to ignore each other *(and affecting lament)* **sob, sob, and double sob!**

(Jake turns to look at Sally. Sally turns to Jake. As soon as their eyes meet, again they turn their backs to each other.)

Voice over - Once upon a time, there was a lonely little girl who ignored the lonely little boy in the hope of finding someone else!

(Sally turns to the audience and peers out as if looking for someone. Finding no-one turns to find that Jake is looking at her. As soon as their eyes meet, Sally turns her back to Jake.)

Pause

Voice over – Once upon a time, there was a lonely little boy who ignored the lonely little girl in the hope of finding someone else!

(Jake turns to the audience and peers out as if looking for someone. Finding no-one turns to find that Sally is looking at him. As soon as their eyes meet, Jake turns his back to Sally.)

Voice over - Once upon a time, there was a lonely little girl and a lonely little boy who ignored each other until finding no one else around...

Pause

(Sally turns to Jake, Jake turns to Sally, their eyes meet, Sally smiles, Jake turns to the audience and indicates exuberant delight,)

Voice over - Hooray!

(Jake looks up to see where that sound came from. Finding nothing, turns back to Sally (still smiling) and smiles back. Both, still smiling, vacillate between looking at the audience and each other.)

Pause

Jake – *(takes two steps towards Sally, and sings all the while looking at Sally)* **Lavender's blue, dilly, dilly,**

Sally – *(takes two steps towards Jake, and sings all the while looking at Jake)* **Lavender's green,**

Jake – *(sings all the while looking at Sally)* **When I am king, dilly, dilly,**

Sally – *(sings all the while looking at Jake)* **I shall be queen.**

Jake – *(sings all the while looking at Sally)* **Who told you so, dilly, dilly, who told you so?**

Sally – *(sings all the while looking at Jake)* **'Twas my own heart, dilly, dilly, my heart told me so.**

Jake – *(takes two steps towards Sally, and sings all the while looking at Sally.)* **Lavender's green, dilly, dilly,**

Sally – *(takes two steps towards Sally, and sings all the while looking at Sally)* **Lavender's blue,**

Jake – *(sings all the while looking at Jake)* **If you love me, dilly, dilly,**

Sally – *(sings all the while looking at Sally)* **I will love you.**

Jake – *(sings all the while looking at Jake)* **Who told you so, dilly, dilly, who told you so?**

Sally – *(sings all the while looking at Sally)* **'Twas my own heart, dilly, dilly, my heart told me so.** *(Sally takes two steps towards Jake, and sings all the while looking at Jake)* **I love to dance, dilly, dilly,**

Jake – *(takes two steps towards Sally, and sings all the while looking at Sally)* **I love to sing, dilly, dilly,**

Sally – *(sings all the while looking at Jake)* **I'll be your**

queen, dilly, dilly,

Jake – *(sings all the while looking at Sally)* **I'll be your**

king.

(Jake & Sally walk until they both reach the centre parting of the curtain, and sing, both looking at each other.)

Sally – Who told you so, dilly, dilly,

Jake - Who told you so?

Jake – I told myself, dilly, dilly,

Sally – I told me so.

(Both turn to face the curtain, tentatively reach out to hold hands, turn to face each other, smile, turn their heads to smile back at the audience, part the curtain and walk through onto the stage behind the curtains.)

Voice over – Once upon a time, there was a lonely

little girl and a lonely little boy who ignored

each other and, finding no one else around,

became friends. *(and sings)*

Lavender's green dilly, dilly, Lavender's

Blue. If you love me, dilly, dilly, I will love
you.

SCENE I

(Curtain rises to reveal two square wooden tables. One table is set at the left side of the stage and the other table is set in the middle of the stage with the two chairs placed on either side of that table so that the actors sit across the table, in profile to the audience. The table on the side of the stage has an electric kettle of hot water, a mug, box of tea bags and a jar of coffee. Charles, dressed in jeans and a T-shirt and shoes indicating that he has been outside, is sitting at the table in the centre of the stage, drinking coffee. He is reading an agony column in a women's magazine.)

Jake – *(Speaking to himself)* **God, I can't believe the stuff they write about! Everything's about me, me, me. Is that what they think having a relationship's about? They talk of love as if only** *they* **know what it means. Why don't they ask me, I'd tell them! I'd tell them love is about...well...it's simple really...yes, dead simple, it's about ...ok...** *(despairing)* **I don't know what love is! I mean,** *(flustered)* **it's what you read about...it's got nothing to do with real life!**

In real life, love is...

'Love me when I want you to,

Love me how I want you to,

Love me as long as I want you to,

and then, bugger off. I need me time!'

That's love; a selfish emotion shrouded by a veil of selflessness. Tear away the shroud and you're left with the unkindness of truth.

(Pause)

She asks, 'Why should I love you?' and, he answers, 'because *I* love you!' So, trade love for love and stay in love for as long as we can trade, or, in time, as opportunities fade, we reconcile ourselves to the last trade we've made.

(Pause)

God, what the hell am I talking about! What am I doing here? Drinking coffee in her flat, coffee which I had to buy because she doesn't drink coffee, reading a women's magazine. Full of self-righteousness for an act of misguided kindness. I came here because I'm a friend. A good friend, a kind friend, a friend in need. A bloody friend! A bloody friend who looks on while she screws up her life trying to find someone to fall in love with. God! This is so stupid!

(Jake starts flicking through the magazine, his mind clearly elsewhere. He gets to the end of the magazine and throws it on the table in disgust!)

One day, I swear....one day! Oh, fuck it!

There'll never be one day! I'll keep doing this

for ever!

(Stands, walks around, visibly calms down, sits back in his chair, opens the magazine, finds the column he was reading and starts reading again. As he reads, he starts humming the tune of Lavender's blue, thinks as he

hums, trying to remember the words and, remembering them, starts singing softly to himself.)

Lavender's blue, dilly, dilly, lavender's green,

When I am king, dilly, dilly, you shall be queen.

Who told you so, dilly, dilly, who told you so?

(Pause – he's can't remember the next line, and then satisfied at his cleverness he makes up the next line.)

Who the fuck knows, dilly, dilly, who the fuck knows?

(Jake hums the tune to himself while continuing to read and, after humming a couple of bars, continues to sing.)

When I am king, dilly, dilly, you shall be queen...

(Jake continues humming the tune to himself while reading and, after humming a couple of bars, continues to sing.)

Lavender's green, dilly, dilly, Lavender's

blue,

If you love me, dilly, dilly, I will love you.

And if you don't, dilly, dilly, and if you don't.

Who the fuck cares, dilly, dilly, who the fuck

cares!

(Sally walks onto stage wearing a tracksuit bottoms and a t-shirt.)

Sally – What are you so happy about?

Jake – *(Looks up, pauses, smiles, and sings to*

Sally tenderly.) **when I am king,**

dilly, dilly, you shall be...

Sally – Oh, cut the crap!

Jake – Hi.

Sally – Hi.

Jake – *(points to the magazine)* **I was just**

looking through what you women

write about.

Sally – What?

Jake – To agony aunts!

Sally – *(Demonstrably not interested.)* **Oh.**

(Sally walks around the kitchen looking for something.)

Jake – **I can't believe you go through all this stuff but never let on to boyfriends or husbands etc.**

Sally – *(Still looking for something.)* **Yeah, especially bloody *Etcetera's***

Jake – **What?**

Sally – **Etcetera's, those sons of bitches who screw you and then piss off!**

Jake – *(Jake quizzically)* **You mean like one night-stands?**

Sally – **No, worse.**

Jake – **How's the head?**

(Sally walks up to table and takes a seat. She is clearly suffering from a hangover. Jake stares at her as she does so.)

Jake – **God, you look awful.**

Sally – **Thanks.**

Jake – Feeling better?

Sally – Than being dead, yeah, suppose. Wish I was!

Jake – What?

Sally – Dead!

Jake – There wouldn't be much point. Too late to

find out which was better.

Sally – What?

Jake – Whether it's better being alive than dead.

Sally – Oh, God, gimme a break!

(Sally throws her head into her hands, demonstrably suffering from the aftermath of a hangover.)

Jake – I made some coffee.

Sally – *(Sally looks up at Jake)* Coffee? Where did

you find it?

Jake – I popped out to get some while you were

asleep.

Sally – *(to herself but loud enough to be heard)* I don't

like coffee.

Jake – I know. Your mug has a tea bag in it. English

Breakfast, OK?

Sally – Thanks. *(Sally walks up to the other table, takes the kettle and pours water into her mug and resumes her seat. Takes a sip.) (To herself)* **That's good.**

Jake - How are you feeling?

Sally – Tired.

Jake – I'm not surprised.

Sally – Yeah, well...

Jake – You didn't sleep much.

Sally – I don't remember sleeping at all. *(then looking up at him)* **Thanks for coming by last night.**

Jake – That's OK.

Sally – You didn't get much sleep either.

Jake – That's OK.

Sally – Aren't you going to work?

Jake – Are you?

Sally – In this state? Nah, I don't think so. Aren't

you?

Jake – Yes *(thinks, changes his mind)* **I mean no.**

Sally – Why not?

Jake – Don't feel great.

Sally – Won't you get into trouble?

Jake – Nah, I'll be alright.

Sally – You sure?

Jake – Yes, I'd rather stay here to make sure you're OK.

Sally – No, it's O.K., I'm fine.

Jake – I'd rather stay.

(Sally stares at him, thinks.)

Sally – You're nice, did I ever tell you that?

(Jake sticks his tongue out at her.)

Sally – No, seriously! I don't know why you don't find someone who deserves you.

Jake – Nah, I'm OK.

Sally – You should.

Jake – I will.

Sally – No, I mean it. There's someone out there
who really needs you. You can't spend your
life looking after sluts like me. I mean, I'm
really glad you came over and everything,
but you need someone, someone special.
God if I found someone like you, I'd never
let them go!

Jake – Yeah, well, shit happens.

Sally – (*Not registering his comment*) If that bloody
Charlie was half as good as you I'd do
anything for him.

Jake – Forget him. He's not worth it.

Sally – I know. I don't know why I always fall for
guys like that! Son of a bitch!

Jake – Don't beat yourself up about him. He's not
worth it! There're many good guys out there.
You just have to wait until the right one

comes along.

Sally – It's easy for you to say.

Jake – No, I mean it. There're plenty of guys out
there.

Sally – Where? You know the bastards I've met.
Every single one of them...each one treated
me like shit!

Jake – Stop it!

Sally – No, really, every single one of them. Get
what they're after and, when they're done,
they're looking for an excuse to bugger off.
Don't even have the courage to even say,
'Thanks love, it was good while it lasted but
time to move on.' Spineless gits leave you
thinking it was all your fault.

Jake – Well, you just have to wait till you find the
one you're looking for.

Sally – *(to herself)* I thought that was Charlie.

Jake – Oh stop it, for God's sake!

Sally – *(with more emphasis)* **No, I really thought this time, just for once I'd found someone who could make me happy. I'd give him what he wanted, and the rest. I'd cook and clean for him. Do anything!**

(Jake visibly thinking about something.)

Sally – **What's the matter?**

Jake – **Nothing.**

Sally – **No, don't look all sad. Everything's gonna be fine. I've got you to look after me, haven't I? You've always been there for me. You'll always be there for me, won't you?**

Jake – **Yes, of course I will, but I wish you wouldn't go on about it. We talked about it all night!**

Sally – **My head hurts.**

Jake – Not surprised, you'd downed half a bottle of vodka before I got here.

Sally – Well you took long enough to get here!

Jake – So now it's my fault!

Sally – **No. I'm sorry** *(thinks, changes her mind)* **Well yes, actually it is.**

Jake – How's that?

Sally – If you were with someone you wouldn't be here. She wouldn't let you go out in the middle of the night to look after some slutty friend who's fucked up again!

Jake – You're crazy.

Sally – You too.

Jake – Just shut up and drink your coffee!

Sally – *(with affected sarcasm)* **Tea, actually.**

Jake – Ha ha.

(Pause)

Sally – No, seriously. You need to find someone.

Jake – I will.

Sally – How? Sitting in that lousy apartment of yours waiting for someone to knock on the door.

Jake – *(visibly irritated)* Yeah, well, you're one to talk.

Sally – Thanks.

Jake – Sorry. I didn't mean it. You're right. I'm getting mad because you're right. I need to find someone. I will. It's just every relationship I've had that I cared about wasn't normal.

Sally – there isn't such a thing as a normal relationship?

Jake – Hmm...Maybe.

Sally – But you need to get out there, dating agencies n stuff. You can't wait around for someone to turn up.

Jake – I know, you said. But I've tried dating agencies.

Sally – You never told me!

Jake – Yes, well, it's not something you throw into a conversation. You know, 'Hey, guess what? I've registered with a dating agency. Wait for it, folks, the series in which shitface! Moi *(pointing to himself)*, has disastrous dates with desperate women.'

Sally – What happened?

Jake – Nothing much. Had two dates. The first one, I paid a fortune to listen to a marketing executive who told me she didn't have time for dates which is why she would get right to the point. Then she spent the next two hours guzzling most of the wine, playing around with the food she had taken an embarrassingly long time to order, while

telling me what she expected of the man
who was lucky enough to have her.

When I didn't call her, she sent me a text
telling me what a loser I was.

Sally – Did you reply?

Jake – Yes, of course. I told her I hoped she'd find
someone who was desperate enough for
what she had to offer.

Sally – What was her reaction?

Jake – She reported me to the agency who said that
they did not expect clients to be rude
and therefore had to cancel my
registration.

Sally – Can they do that? What about the money
you paid?

Jake – Apparently, they can. I lost the money. It
was all in the small print.

Sally – I thought you said you had two.

Jake – Yes, well. The second one was awful.

Sally – How?

Jake – She moaned about everything. She kept saying how she didn't want to be there, which, of course, made me feel great! It was the most painful hour of my life.

Sally – And?

Jake – Nothing. The agency wrote saying she'd cancelled her membership, but said they had lots more to choose from. I told them 'thanks, but no thanks.'

Sally – That's shit!

Jake – Yeah, well. At least I tried.

(Pause, while both drink. Sally is looking and feeling a lot better.)

Sally – Listen. I've got an idea.

Jake – What?

Sally – You know I told you I went to a speed dating thing last month. Remember, before I met Charlie.

Jake – No thanks.

Sally – No, just hear me out.

Jake – No! I'd rather hang myself!

Sally – Why?

Jake – Admit to becoming one of those lonely bastards who are so desperate they resort to that kind of thing. I tried the dating agency. At least they do something to match you up.

Sally – That's bullshit. You can't get computers to sort out chemistry. Computers deal with hard facts!

Jake – Well, that's not what the adverts say.

Sally – Are you gonna tell me you believe that bullshit!

Jake – Well it can't all be bullshit. It works for some.

Sally – God, you're so…

Jake - Yes, well, why is speed dating any better?

Sally – At least you can leave it to chance!

Jake – Meaning chance is better than computers?

Sally – Random.

Jake – What?

Sally – Random…you know…chance.

Jake – *(not really sure he understands)* **Oh.**

Sally – Look, I think you should give it a go.

Jake – Didn't work for you!

Sally – Yes, well it was an off day. You don't get lucky every time. And, anyway, I don't have trouble meeting guys.

Jake – Yes, I know.

Sally – OK, no need to be a bastard!

Jake – I'm not doing it.

Sally – Don't be such an ass.

Jake – You mean arse! *(Emphasising the R)*

Sally – Yeah, well, whatever!

Jake – I'm still not doing it!

Sally – Look you can't go on like this.

Jake – Like what?

Sally – Like this. Looking after useless girls who use you for a shoulder to cry on whenever some bastard dumps them.

Jake – Oh shut up!

Sally – No, I won't shut up. It's the truth and you've got to hear it.

Jake – I'm not listening.

Sally – Well, you're just gonna have to!

Jake – I told you, I'm not listening. *(shuts his ears)*

Sally – How long have I known you?

Jake – I'm not listening.

Sally – *(louder)* How long?

Jake – *(thinks)* **Two years.**

Sally – **And do you remember the first time we met.**

Jake – **Don't....**

Sally – **You pulled that bastard off me.**

Jake – **Please don't.**

Sally – **No, remember how they laughed when he was on top of me. Fucking prats! They wanted to see him fuck me. My screaming didn't stop him. He was laughing. They all were.**

Jake – **Yeah, well. You were drunk too.**

Sally – **I know, but I didn't say he could have a go.**

Jake – **Getting drunk isn't fun all the time.**

Sally – **You were the only one to help. And you cleaned up the mess when you brought me home. Even though I wasn't really all there, I remember lying in bed hearing you retch as you cleaned up my sick!**

Jake – Do you have to?

Sally – When I awoke, you were sleeping on the floor beside me.

Jake – Yeah, I was afraid you'd choke on your sick.

Sally – And I woke you up…

Jake – Yeah, I remember, you cow! Laughing at me.

Sally – Well, it was your fault. You looked so funny with the black eye you brought home with you. Black, no, purple. It was amazing. All I could think of was seeing you go to work with that black eye.

Jake – They had a laugh when I got to the office.

Sally – I'm not surprised.

Jake – Yeah, well, you don't always get a black eye for taking a girl home!

Sally – You're crazy!

Jake – So are you!

(Pause)

Sally – You know, you need to find a girl worth having a black eye over.

Jake – I have thanks. One's enough! Two would blind me.

Sally – You're mad!

Jake – You too.

(Pause)

Sally – Anyway, as I was saying. You need to find a girlfriend.

Jake – I will.

Sally – No, I mean someone serious.

Jake – Oh, now I suppose they come in categories. In accordance with the Trade Descriptions Act, blah blah blah, each girl is required by law to forewarn predatory males, the extent to which they are fit for purpose, clearly stating, in a clear and unambiguous manner whether they are available for just a one-night stand, trial period, with a money back guarantee, or for non-refundable, serious intent!

Sally – Why do you always have to act so clever?

Jake – Only when you are being stupid!

Sally – Idiot!

Jake – Takes one to know one!

Sally – Big kid!

(Jake sticks his tongue out at her.)

(Pause)

Sally – So?

Jake – So what?

Sally – You gonna do it?

Jake – Do what?

Sally – Try it?

Jake – What are you on about now?

Sally – Speed dating, twit face!

Jake – No!

Sally – Why not?

Jake – I said, 'No.' Which part of the word 'No' don't you understand!

Sally – *(with emphasis)* **Why not?**

Jake – Why can't women take 'No' for an answer.

Sally – *(Laughs)* **It's usually men that can't take 'No' for an answer.**

Jake – Yeah, well, I'm not talking about sex!

(Sally, ignoring the allusion to sex, continues.)

Sally – Come on, why not?

Jake – Look, I just don't want to.

Sally – Just for fun?

Jake – Why don't you do it?

Sally – I told you, I don't have any trouble finding men!

Jake – Yeah, well, they can't be any worse than the one's you find!

Sally – Bastard!

(Pause)

Jake – Sorry. *(Stands, walks over to her, and puts his arms around her. She shrugs it away. Repeats, shrugs it away but this time with less determination. Jake caresses her back.)*

Jake – I'm sorry.

Sally – *(with irritation)* **OK, OK, just sit down and drink your coffee.**

(Jake walks back to his chair and sits down.)

Jake – I didn't mean it, but you keep going on and on.

Sally – Look, you're one of the nicest friends I've got and all I want is for you to be happy.

Jake – I am.

Sally – Are you?

Jake – Yeah, sure. Why, don't I look it?

(Sally looks at him, shrugs unconvinced.)

Jake – When the time's right, the right girl will
come along.

Sally – But she won't come knocking on your door
like the 'Avon Lady'

Jake – Why, don't they still come around?

Sally – How the hell should I know?

Jake – Oh well. Now I know why I haven't found the
right girl! I thought they were on strike or
something!

Sally – What?

Jake – The Avon ladies!

Sally – You're crazy!

Jake – You said that already.

Sally – I know. Just reminding you, twit face.

Jake – You said that too!

(Sally sighs in despair.)

(Pause)

Sally – So, you gonna do it?

Jake – *(speaking to himself)* **It's no use.** *(Then to her.)*

I thought CDs couldn't be scratched.

Sally – What?

Jake – You know, CD's, you can't scratch CD's?

(Sally looks at him quizzically.)

Jake – You know, broken record! Going on and on.

Never mind.

(Sally in a huff, turns away conveying to him that she is ignoring him.)

Jake – Come on, don't get in a huff.

(Ignores him)

Jake – Please!

Sally – OK, so will you?

(Sally waits while Jake thinks)

Sally – Come on you can do this. Do it for me.

Jake – *(thinks, staring at her)* **OK, I'll do it... only...**

Sally – Only what?

Jake – Only if you do it too.

Sally – Don't be stupid.

Jake – Well that's the deal. Take it or leave it.

Sally – Why would I want to do that?

Jake – Because *(aping her voice)* **'you're my friend
and want me to be happy.'**

(Sally thinks)

Sally – Nah!

Jake – Oh I see, it's OK for me to do it because you
say so, but not the other way around?

(Sally thinks. Jake stares at her.)

Sally – OK. I'll come with you.

Jake – No, that's not good enough.

Sally – Come on, be fair!

Jake – No, you have to do it too.

Sally – But I don't want to meet anyone. Not just
yet.

Jake – Fine, we'll wait.

Sally – *(pleading)* **No, you go on, please. I need time
to get over Charlie.**

Jake – I'm in no rush. I said I'll do it and I mean it.

We both can do it when you're ready.

(Sally thinks.)

Sally – OK, I'll do it.

Jake – You will?

Sally – Yes.

Jake – You sure?

Sally – Yes.

Jake – OK, I'll find an event.

Sally – No, it's OK. I'll find one.

Jake – No.

Sally – *(with emphasis)* I said, I'll find something. If I leave it to you, it'll take forever. Anyway, I think I know of one.

Jake – Really, how?

Sally – Kris at work was telling me about one.

Jake – Kris?

Sally – You don't know her.

(Jake looks interested.)

Sally – No, she's not your type.

Jake – How can you tell?

Sally – I know your type.

Jake – Really, go on, then. What's my type?

Sally – That's easy.

(Sally thinks.)

Jake – Go on.

Sally – I'm thinking.

Jake – Can't be that easy if you need to think about it.

Sally – I'm thinking about where to start. *(thinks)* **Hair, the same colour as mine but a little longer. About the same height and build. Maybe a little bigger on the bum and tits.**

Jake – Stand up.

Sally – What?

Jake – Just stand up, will you!

(Sally stands up.)

Jake – Turn around.

(Sally turns around.)

Jake - No, yours are fine.

Sally – You mean height and build, right? *(As she sits down with a mischievous smile.)*

Jake – *(smiling)* **Yes, of course.**

Sally – Never know with you sometimes.

Jake – What do you mean? *(Realising what she's thinking)* **Don't be silly.**

Sally – OK, just checking. After all, you have put me to bed more than once.

Jake – You forgot, last night it was not just your clothes. Had to wash the sick out of your hair too!

Sally – OK, let's change the subject.

Jake – Sorry.

Sally – *(thinks)* **Was it really that bad?**

(Jake nods.)

Sally – What did you do with my clothes.

Jake – I put them on the radiator in the bedroom.

(Sally gets up, walks over, and kisses him on the head.)

Sally – You're really special, do you know that.

Really special… *(she repeats as if to herself)*

Jake – OK, that's enough. Drink your coffee.

Sally – Tea. Anyway, I'm going to have a shower.

Jake – OK, when you're ready, I take you out for

some breakfast.

Sally – That sounds good. Where?

Jake – Same place?

Sally – Yeah, same place.

(Sally leaves the stage and Jake sits for a while, gets up, picks up her mug and his, looks around and walks off stage with them. We are left with an empty stage. Lights dim into total darkness.)

Curtain Falls

SCENE II

(Lights go back on. Sally enters stage dressed to go out. Looks at her phone. Puts phone back on the table. Sally wanders impatiently around the stage. Goes back to the table and sits down. Jake enters stage with a change of T-shirt or something indicating he is ready for the speed dating event.)

Sally – Thought you'd chickened out!

Jake – Thought about it.

Sally – Lucky for you, you didn't!

Jake – *(being silly)* **Ooo, I'm scared.**

Sally – Oh grow up!

(Jake stops being silly.)

Sally – So, ready?

Jake – No!

Sally – Oh stop being such a wimp!

Jake – I think you're turning me into a wimp!

Sally – What do you mean?

Jake – This bloody speed dating idea of yours.

Sally – I'm gonna do it too.

Jake – Yes, well, you need someone. I don't!

Sally – I think it's the other way around. You're the one who needs to find someone. If anything, I'm the one who needs a break.

Jake – Yeah, well, why don't we both enjoy having a break being single together? Why go through all that again?

Sally – Again?

Jake – Yes, again!

Sally – 'Again' implies that you've been making a habit of it.

Jake – Habit of what?

Sally – Falling in love!

Jake – Yes, well, neither of us are virgins!

Sally – *(laughs)* That's one way of putting it.

Jake – Yeah, too right. Scars to prove it.

Sally – Who hasn't. But that doesn't mean you have to go teetotal. Like the ads say, 'drink sensibly'.

Jake – I don't think you can apply that to falling in
love.

Sally – You can.

Jake – And how do you propose doing that?

Sally – Just don't get carried away. Fall in love
sensibly.

Jake – *(sarcastically)* **And *you're* going to tell me
how.**

Sally – Yes. And you can cut out the sarcasm.
You're not good at it!

Jake – I wasn't being...

Sally – *(cutting him off)* **Yes, you were.**

Jake – OK, maybe a little.

Sally – You know what they say about teaching.

Jake – Teaching?

Sally – Yes, teaching.

Jake – What?

Sally – 'Do as I say, don't do as I do.'

Jake – OK, how?

Sally – Don't start dreaming from the first date on. Just take it easy. If it's going to happen it will in its own time. Just, go with the flow.

Jake – You're full of....

Sally – You're dead!

Jake – What?

Sally – Say what you were going to say, and you're dead!

Jake – I was going to say, full of... wisdom.

Sally – *(Laughs.)* Yeah, right!

Jake – I was.

Sally – And saying I was full of shit didn't cross your mind!

Jake – No it didn't!

Sally – Prat!

Jake – Muppet!

(Both laugh.)

Sally – We're like a couple of kids!

Jake – Yeah, well, maybe we'll be lucky and never grow up.

Sally – OK, enough stalling. You ready?

Jake – No.

Sally – Good. Neither am I.

Jake – What do we have to do?

Sally – Nothing. I've done it.

Jake – Done what?

Sally – I've made the preparations.

Jake – What preparations?

Sally – I paid and gave them your email.

Jake – You mean, *our* emails?

Sally – Yeah, yeah, our emails!

(Pause)

Jake – What if there's someone I know or who knows me?

Sally – Will you stop it? You're not that important. And, even if there is, they're in the same boat as you.

Jake – Yeah, I suppose so. What else did you tell them?

Sally – Nothing. They keep your contact details confidential. When you get there,   you're given a number and basically, that's that! Girls sit at the table, and guys move around at the sound of the buzzer.

Jake – How long do we have?

Sally – Four minutes.

Jake – *(sarcastically)* Four minutes to find the love of our lives.

Sally – There you go again.

Jake – What?

Sally – No-one's talking about finding love n stuff!

Jake – Then what's the point?

Sally – Look, stop it! No point being miserable all over again.

Jake – I'm not.

Sally – Yes you are.

Jake – I didn't say a word.

Sally – You don't have to.

Jake – Uh?

Sally – You don't have to say anything. All people have to do is look at you and they know what you were thinking. You have to be careful. Especially if you're talking to girls. We have very sensitive antennae.

Jake – Is that what you call them?

Sally – What?

Jake – *(looking at her breasts)* **Antennae.**

Sally – Oh shut up! Anyway, let's be serious.

(pause) **So you need to sort out what you're**

going to do to impress her in under four minutes.

(Jake still smiling)

Oh, be serious for God's sake!

Jake – *(laughing)* **Look, how can you be serious about speed dating. Do you really think you can find someone worth having on a four-minute date?**

Sally – It's not about 'having' someone, it's about making a start! You meet so many people and time passes so quickly and, unless the organisers fall asleep, you won't have time to remember much about any of them. That's the whole point. It's an icebreaker.

Jake – Why did you do it?

Sally – What do you mean?

Jake – Nothing, I just didn't figure you as being someone who'd go to a speed dating thing and you never told me. When was it?

Sally – Never mind.

Jake – No, now you've got me interested.

Sally – I don't want to talk about it.

Jake – Why not?

Sally – This is about you, not me.

Jake – But I wanna to know?

Sally – Maybe some other time.

Jake – When?

Sally – Sometime.

Jake – That means never, right?

Sally – No, it means sometime. If you go on it'll mean never!

Jake – OK.

Sally – So?

Jake – *(pleading)* **Look, I really don't want to.**

Sally – I know. But it's for your own good.

Jake – How's that?

Sally – You need to get back in the game. You've

been out too long. You really need to get

your confidence back again.

Jake – OK... but you're coming with me, right?

Sally – Yes. I said I would.

Jake – No, I mean you're going to do it too.

Sally – Look, stop being a baby.

Jake – No! If you're not going to do it, I'm not doing

it either. And that's final!

Sally – You're such a Wuss!

Jake – You can call me what you want, but

that's the deal.

Sally – *(exasperated)* **Look, I said I will!**

Jake – That's good.

Sally – So, you need to think about what you're

going to say.

Jake – About what?

Sally – About yourself, stupid!

Jake – Don't we just ask questions?

Sally – It depends.

Jake – On what?

Sally – On who you meet, stupid! Whether the girl
wants to tell you about herself or wants to
find out about you. *(Sally looks askingly)*

Jake – What?

Sally – What are you gonna say?

Jake – About what?

Sally – Are you just acting dumb?

Jake – I really don't want to do this.

Sally – Why not?

Jake – It's stupid.

Sally – It's not.

Jake – Look, I'll just go along and play it by ear.

Sally – You can't do that.

Jake – Why not?

Sally – Because you've only got four minutes!

Jake – You're making it sound like life or death.

Sally – Well, you've got to think about what you're gonna say upfront, otherwise you'll only mumble.

Jake – I don't mumble.

Sally – Yes, you do.

Jake – Did you practice?

Sally – Yes.

Jake – OK, then, let's hear it then.

Sally – No, it's about you.

Jake – I know, but if I hear what you'd say, I'd get some idea of what I should say.

Sally – Hmm.

Jake – What?

Sally – You're a devious bugger, but OK.

(Pause)

Jake – Go on then.

Sally – OK. Wait a minute.

(Jake waits. They look at each other.)

Sally – My name is Sally. *(thinks)* I'm thirty-two years old. I work in HR. I like going out… rock climbing, skiing, eating out, films. I live in Fulham. I went to Sussex Uni. Oh! I dunno. Something like that!

Jake – Well, if anyone says, 'Why don't you tell me about yourself for two minutes,' I think I'll puke! I mean, how anal can you get?

Sally – Yeah, I suppose so. *(Laughs)* Actually, I can't remember what the hell I said!

Jake – Did you get a second date?

Sally – Yeah, I got three.

Jake – *(impressed)* Three?

Sally – Yeah.

Jake – How many of you were there?

Sally – I dunno, maybe thirty.

Jake – Is that good?

Sally – What?

Jake – Three dates out of thirty?

Sally – No stupid. There were 15 guys and 15 girls.

Jake – So it lasted for an hour.

Sally – Why?

Jake – Four minutes per couple.

Sally – Yes, I suppose so, but it felt longer.

Jake – Why?

Sally – I dunno. A lot of waiting around.

Jake – What did you do afterwards?

Sally – Nothing. Just went home.

Jake – Did you end up meeting all the guys you
wanted to?

Sally – No. You don't because you both have to want
to meet each other.

Jake – How many did you want to meet?

Sally – *(Thinks.)* I can't remember. I think at the time I was scared no one would pick me so I marked anyone who was half decent.

Jake – What do you mean?

Sally – You know. I just marked 'yes' to anyone who didn't look like a complete nerd.

Jake – I can't believe you did that.

Sally – *(Laughs)* I know. I still can't.

Jake – What made you do it?

Sally – I don't know. I just felt I had to. I was tired of being set up with someone.
Friends think they're doing you a favour just because they've set you up with someone.

Jake – Yeah, that's true.

Sally – Anyway, I just got fed up of it. I wanted to find someone myself. Someone not associated with friends. Someone I could secretly try out so that when things didn't work out, I'd be spared all the affected sympathy. Don't get me wrong, I think friends are great but, sometimes, sympathy hurts.

Jake – Yeah, I know what you mean.

Sally – You know, one of the weirdest things I saw at the speed dating thing was most of the people came with someone, you know, like a friend or something for moral support!

Jake – Were they old?

Sally - No. Mixed. From twenty-something's right up to forty something's.

Jake – Outcasts!

Sally – No, not outcasts, just people wanting to meet other people.

Jake – For love?

Sally – I don't think it's about love anymore. I mean, we all want to fall in love, but I think after a while you just get tired of waiting for your knight in shining armour, white steed 'n' all. It's just about finding someone.

Jake – Yeah. I know what you mean.

Sally – I mean, for God's sake, what's wrong with bloody men!

Jake – What do you mean?

Sally – I mean, all the good ones are taken, and the rest of them are either gay or bastards!

Jake – Hang on!

Sally – What? *(then realising)* No, I don't mean you, silly. You're different. You're in a category all of your own.

Jake – Hmm, OK, I'll let you off that one. So, what were the ones at the speed dating like?

Sally – Nothing really... I mean, just normal. Not ugly, not stunning, well... there were a couple who looked pretty good and I wondered why they ended up in a place like that.

Jake – Why, what was wrong with them?

Sally – Nothing. Actually, I was quite excited as I waited for them to get around to me. The three or four no hopers who came before were boring. All they did was talk about themselves. These, I was sure, would be different.

Jake – You were sure?

Sally – OK, I was hoping.

Jake – Poor you. It's awful to hope isn't it.

Sally – What?

Jake – I mean hoping that someone you like might be interested in you.

Sally – Yeah, well. *(thinks)* Why, has that happened to you?

Jake – Sort of.

Sally – What do you mean?

Jake – Nothing.

Sally – Why, do you fancy someone?

Jake – Maybe.

Sally – Who?

Jake – Never mind.

(Sally looks quizzically at Jake.)

So, what happened?

Sally – When?

Jake – The good-looking guys at the speed dating.

Sally – Well one was a complete narcissist. Kept posing for the whole four minutes. When I thought about it later, I couldn't remember what we'd talked about.

(Jake smiles.)

Sally – What?

Jake – Nothing.

Sally – No, what?

Jake – You obviously fancied him.

Sally – You know you're such an idiot! It's one thing
to fancy someone, totally another to want to
get to know them.

Jake – The same applies to getting to know
someone but not fancying them.

Sally – Yes, same thing. Both are lost causes.

Jake – I don't know. I don't believe in love at first
sight and all that crap! I think you grow to
love someone as you get to know them.

Sally – Yes, but that's different. Loving someone
because you like them and loving someone
because you fancy them, they're different.

Jake – Why?

Sally – Well, the first means that you miss out on
all the wild stuff when you're younger, but
the compensation is that you can be friends.

And with the other, you have to find
something to replace the wild stuff when it's
not as exciting as it was.

Jake – You mean you're screwed both ways.

Sally – What?

Jake – Neither is worth having?

(Sally thinks)

Never mind. So, what was the second one
like?

Sally – What?

Jake – The other guy you fancied.

Sally – He was smooth. I was so excited I put two
crosses by his name.

Jake – And?

Sally – Nothing. The fuckwit didn't fancy me.
Maybe I should have shown him more of
what I've got to offer.

Jake – That might have worked.

Sally – Yes, well, he would have to do a lot more
than be smooth for me to put on a show.

Jake – Oh well, c'est la vie!

Sally – Yeah, well, you can stop gloating!

Jake – I'm not.

Sally – It's different for men. You don't have to tart
yourself up to be noticed.

Jake – No? So, what do we have to do?

Sally – Nothing.

Jake – It's not that easy.

Sally – Yes, it is! You just have to go up to someone
and, if you don't get a bite, move on to the
next one.

Jake – Why, can't girls do the same?

Sally – Because that's what guys call a slut! You
think just because you are looking   for   a
good lay, we must be too.

Jake – Good lays are hard to get.

Sally – Actually, it's not a good lay you're after.
It's any lay.

Jake – That's not true.

Sally – Yes, it is!

Jake – That's what you lot think.

Sally – So are you telling me that if a girl was ready
to sleep with you, you'd say, 'No?'

Jake – Yeah, sure!

Sally – That's crap!

Jake – This is stupid!

Sally – What is?

Jake – This conversation.

Sally – Yeah, well you started it.

Jake – No I didn't.

Sally – Yes, you did.

Jake – You're the one who keeps going on
and on about how important it is to meet
someone.

Sally – Yes, well, you have to. You can't go through life feeling sorry for yourself.

Jake – I'm not feeling sorry for myself.

Sally – Sounds like someone is, and it isn't me!

Jake – I'm happy being single.

Sally – I didn't say you need to get married. Just meet someone that you might enjoy spending time with. You know, going out n stuff.

Jake – I have friends.

Sally – Yes, I know. But if you wait forever you won't have any single friends left. They'll all be married or living with someone and, if they stay friends, they'll be forever setting you up with someone.

Jake – There're millions of people who live on their own.

Sally – Yes, but not from choice.

Jake – That's a cruel way of looking at it. Not everyone's destined to be with someone. Some people are happy being on their own.

Sally – Well the one I'm looking at isn't one of them!

Jake – Since when did you become a psychologist!

Sally – Since I met you!

Jake – Ha ha, very funny. Enjoying being a bitch, do you?

Sally – With you hunnybun, always!

Jake – Anyway, you're wrong!

Sally – OK. If you say so.

Jake – I'm happy with my life.

Sally – Looking after girls that can't look after themselves!

Jake – Oh shut up!

Sally – No, it's true. I'm using you. I always do! Whenever I get into a mess, I call you.

Jake – Don't be stupid.

Sally – I'm not being stupid, and you know it!

Jake – Look, that's what friends are for.

Sally – What, using each other?

Jake – Call it what you want, but you'd do the same

for me too.

Sally – Have I ever?

Jake – Wouldn't you?

Sally – Of course I would, stupid, but that's not the

point! I want you to find   someone   who

deserves you.

Jake – As I said, I'm happy being single.

Sally – Yeah, well, we all say that, but it's not true.

No one likes being alone.

Jake – It's not the same...being single and being

lonely.

Sally – Look, forget it! Maybe you're right and I'm

really the lonely one here.

Jake – Oh, give it a rest!

Sally – But it's true. I meet one sorry bastard after another…(remembers)…at least they don't hit me anymore.

Jake – Well, he didn't come back as he promised he would.

Sally – I think he got scared.

Jake – Not surprised, the state he left you in. I told you we should've called the police!

Sally – *(with remorse)* It wasn't all his fault!

Jake – You know, I don't get you. What are you looking for? I mean, everyone you meet is a head case.

Sally – Yeah, I know. I thought Charlie would be different.

Jake – You think every one of them is going to be different!

Sally – Yeah well, maybe it's just me.

Jake – Oh stop it, for Christ's sake! Let's go and get this over and done with.

Sally – Yeah, lets.

Jake – Who knows, maybe the love of your life is waiting for you. He's getting ready to talk to fifteen girls before he suddenly realises, you're the one he's been waiting for.

Sally – *(noticeably a little nervous)* Yes, well, I hope one of us gets lucky.

Jake – Don't worry, we both will. I promise. *(Sally smiles.)* And with a smile like that they'd have to be blind and stupid not to fall in love the moment they see you.

(Sally walks over to Jake and takes him by the arm and leads him off stage.)

Sally – What would I do without you?

Jake – Just what I was thinking.

(They leave the stage)

SCENE III

(The table all this time at the side of the stage is brought to the middle of the stage close to the other table. The two chairs are placed at right angles to the audience so that Jake & Sally are sitting in profile to the audience, one at each of the two tables, both facing in one direction (i.e. not facing each other). Sally sits behind Jake, so she is looking at Jake's back. Both Jake & Sally separately speak to the other side of the table as if someone's there. They indicate a change in person sitting in the imagined chair opposite by appropriate actions. As the conversation moves from Sally to Jake, the one not having a conversation stares trance-like directly ahead of him/her.)

(Buzzer sounds.)

Voice – OK, ladies. Please take your seats.

(Sally walks around the stage deciding where to take a seat. Jake watches her.)

Voice – Thank you, ladies. OK, gentlemen, please take your seats.

(Jake takes a seat.)

Thank you. And your four minutes start now. Good luck!

Sally – Hi

(Sally mimics interest in what the imaginary person in the chair opposite her is saying, nodding, and smiling at appropriate intervals, but is neither asked anything, nor given a chance to say anything.)

Voice – Thank you ladies and gentlemen. Please change, take your seats and your four minutes start now.

Jake – Hi, my name is Jake.

Yes well... *(nervous laugh)*

No, never, what about you?

I didn't think you had. It's not as easy as it sounds. I'm in advertising. No, Account Manager. I look after clients. What about you?

(Jake bored but affecting interest) **That sounds interesting. You can't have much free time. What do you do when you're not working?**

No, I'm not into classical music.

Yes, it is a shame.

Voice – Thank you ladies and gentlemen. Please change, take your seats.

And your four minutes start now. *(Jake turns back to see Sally; they both smile and then he turns back.)*

Sally – Hi. My name is Sally.

Yes, I work in HR.

No, not recruitment, performance evaluation. It's OK... *(Sally with fixed, affected smile)*

No.

No.

No.

Yes, good luck to you too.

Voice – Thank you ladies and gentlemen. Please change, take your seats.

Your four minutes start now.

(Jake turns back to see Sally. Both roll their eyes in boredom.)

Jake – Hi,

(Imagined conversation takes place.)

Voice – Thank you ladies and gentlemen. Please change, take your seats.

Your four minutes start now.

Sally – Hi,

(Imagined conversation takes place.)

Voice – Thank you ladies and gentlemen. Please change, take your seats. *(Jake gets up and takes the seat opposite Sally)*

Your four minutes start now.

Jake – Hi, how's it going?

Sally – I'm bored.

Jake – Well, you're the one that wanted to come.

Sally – Oh shut up!

Jake – So, anything worth having? *(he asks, looking around the group of participants)*

Sally – Nah, nothing much. What about you?

Jake – Yeah, a pretty good bunch, I suppose.

Sally – *(Sally serious)* **But is there anyone that you fancy?**

Jake – Yeah. I suppose so.

(Looks away from Sally and smiles, as if smiling to a girl seated at another table. Smile broadens as he receives a smile back.)

Sally – *(obviously irritated)* **This isn't a joke! You can't just go out with anyone!**

Jake – I thought that was the idea?

Sally – Well, it isn't! OK?

Jake – But isn't that the point? I mean you said that I shouldn't take it too seriously. Go with the flow, you said.

Sally – Yes, but that doesn't mean you *have* to go out with someone. If you don't really fancy them, then better you don't.

Jake – Why not?

Sally – It's not fair on you.

Jake – I don't mind.

Sally – *(with exasperation)* **It may be OK for you but it's not fair on them! I mean the girls here aren't the sort to play around. They're not the type who go looking for a one-night stand.**

Jake – **I don't know. I've met a couple that look as if they'd be up for it.**

Sally – **But you wouldn't, right?**

Jake – **I dunno.**

Sally – **Oh, for Christ's sake.**

Jake – **OK, no, I wouldn't.**

(Sally looks at Jake suspiciously)

Jake – **No, I mean it, I wouldn't.**

Sally – **You better not!**

Voice – **Thank you ladies and gentlemen. Please change, take your seats...**

Your four minutes start now.

Sally – *(Bored)* **Hi,** *(Sally obviously not interested in the person sitting in front of her and with a voice which reveals her boredom)*

> **Yes.**
>
> *No.*
>
> *No.*
>
> *No.*

Voice – Thank you ladies and gentlemen. I hope you had a good evening. We wish you the best of luck. Please don't forget to hand in your cards.

(Jake & Sally stand up, Jake waits for Sally, they smile at each other and walk off the stage together.)

(Curtain Falls)

SCENE IV

(One table is moved back to the side of the stage and the chairs are positioned across the remaining table as in the earlier kitchen scenes. The electric kettle, the women's magazine, coffee jar, box of tea bags and two mugs are placed on the table. Sally enters the stage holding a purse. Looks around, looks at her watch, picks up the magazine and takes her seat at the table in the centre of the stage. Puts the purse on the table. She flicks through the magazine, doesn't find anything of interest and drops the magazine on the table. She looks at her watch.)

Sally – *(to herself)* **He's always late.** *(looks around her, obviously bored)* **I should be used to it by now. At least that's the only thing.** *(Opens her purse and takes out the card handed to her at the speed dating event which she didn't give in. Looks at it.)* **Oh well, that was a waste of time, wasn't it? I thought seven was a lucky number. I wonder whether he marked me as a prospective date. Hmm, maybe I should have handed in the card. That would have been a laugh, the two of us choosing**

each other. Yeah, but he wouldn't have. And even if he did, he would have done it as a joke. Or, when he found out I'd chosen him he would have thought I chose him as a joke. I wish I had the courage to risk losing him. If I did, I wouldn't wait for him to ask me out, I'd ask him out myself! *(Thinking, as she puts the card back into her purse)* I wonder how many dates he got. *(Laughs)* He said he didn't really fancy any of them. I hope he doesn't just take whoever's available. He's worth more than that! I'd kill the bitch that hurt him!

God, he's so naive!

(Jake walks onto stage)

Jake – Hi, talking to yourself?

Sally – Hi.

Jake – Sorry I'm late.

Sally – That's OK.

Sally – So?

Jake – What?

Sally – How many did dates you get?

Jake – Oh, lots.

Sally – But you said you didn't fancy any of them.

Jake – Well I thought I'd take your advice and get
out there.

Sally – Hang on. You saying it's going to be my
fault?

Jake – What?

Sally – When it doesn't work out you gonna say it
was my fault?

Jake – I haven't met anyone yet!

Sally – Yeah, but when you do...

Jake – Look, I was just kidding.

(Sally looks confused)

I took your advice and decided I would only say 'yes' if I really fancied someone.

Sally – Good.

Jake – So how many did you mark?

Sally – What?

Jake – How many did you say 'yes' to?

Sally – One.

Jake – Why only one?

Sally – Didn't fancy any of the others.

Jake – I thought some of the guys looked your type.

Sally – Really, and what's my type.

Jake – You know, tall, dark, and handsome!

Sally – Creep!

Jake – What?

Sally – You're making fun of me.

Jake – No, I'm not. I've known a lot of your boyfriends and they've all been pretty good looking.

Sally – You turning gay on me?

Jake – No, I'm just saying. *(pause)* **So did the one you like, like you too?**

Sally – No.

Jake – Stupid bastard!

Sally – Yes, I think so too.

Jake – Which one was he?

Sally – Never mind.

Jake – No, tell me.

Sally – I don't want to talk about it.

Jake – OK. God! I'm never going through that again!

Sally – No. Me neither.

Jake – We'll just have to wait till the right one comes along. *(Sally looks as if she's miles away)* **What's the matter?**

Sally – Nothing.

Jake – Don't worry. He probably wasn't worth it.

(Jake notices Sally is looking sad) **No really.**

You'll find someone.

Sally – *(quietly)* **Yeah...No, I won't!**

Jake – Yes, you will.

(As the conversation continues Sally is getting increasingly upset.)

Sally – What makes you so sure?

Jake – I just know.

Sally – No. No-one fancies me.

Jake – That's not true!

Sally – I'm stupid!

Jake – No, you're not!

Sally – Yes, I am. Just good enough for one-night stands!

Jake – How can you say that?

Sally – Cause I'm...fat!

Jake – No, you're not.

Sally – Yes, I am.

Jake – Oh, stop it.

Sally – And sad, and, …ugly!

Jake – For Christ's sake!

Sally – Just a stupid bitch worth a screw! Everyone either hates me or uses me!

(Sally buries face in hands.)

Jake – Oh for Christ's sake, please. Please stop.

(Jake gets up and walks over to her, stands beside her, and puts his arm around her. She turns and hugs him.) **You're not any of those things. No-one could ever hate you. You're just the most amazing girl in the whole fucking world! I swear! I'll always be there for you. I swear I will.**

Sally – *(Looking up at him)* **Promise?**

Jake – Yes, I promise.

Sally – *(Sally looks up at Jake)* **You're crazy.**

Jake – Yeah, I know. You too.

Sally - Made for each other?

Jake - Probably.

Sally – By the way, what number were you at the speed dating?

Jake - Why?

Sally - No, go on!

Jake - Seven, I think.

(Sally opens her purse and gives him her card. He looks at the card, looks at her, they smile tenderly at each other – pause- and then kiss.

(Curtain falls.)